For Thomas and Max with love —S.W.

Copy Me, Copycub
Copyright © 1999 by Frances Lincoln Limited
Text copyright © 1999 by Richard Edwards
Illustrations copyright © 1999 by Susan Winter
Printed in Hong Kong. All rights reserved.
ISBN 0-06-028570-2
Library of Congress catalog card number: 99-1175
http://www.harperchildrens.com
Originally published by Frances Lincoln Limited, 4 Torriano
Mews, Torriano Avenue, London NW5 2RZ, England.

Copy Me, Copycub

by Richard Edwards

pictures by Susan Winter

HARPERCOLLINS*PUBLISHERS*

It was spring in the north woods,
and the bears were out exploring.
    Everything his mother did,
the cub did too.

When his mother splashed through a swamp,
the cub splashed through a swamp.
When his mother sat down for a scratch,
the cub sat down for a scratch.

   "You know what you are," said the mother bear.
"You're a little Copycub."

From spring into summer the bears wandered, looking for good things to eat.

When his mother picked berries, Copycub picked berries.

When his mother climbed a tree for honey, Copycub climbed a tree for honey.

"Yes, you're my own little Copycub," his mother said, giving him a hug.

Autumn came, and the days grew colder. One morning when the bears awoke, there was frost on the ground.

"It's time for us to go to our cave," said the mother bear. "Winter's coming, and soon it'll be too cold to stay outside. The cave will shelter us from the snow. Follow me, Copycub, and keep close behind."

His mother lolloped through the trees.
Copycub lolloped through the trees.

His mother waded streams.
Copycub waded streams.

It was a long journey for a small bear. Copycub tried his best to keep up, but he was beginning to feel very tired when something cold and wet touched the end of his nose.

It was beginning to snow.

Snow fell quickly, snow fell thickly, blowing into Copycub's eyes, so he could hardly see the way. Ice fringed his fur and his paws were numb with cold. He couldn't go one step further. All he wanted to do was lie down and sleep.

But his mother came back for him.

"You can't sleep here, or you'll freeze," she said. "Come on, Copycub, the cave's not far. Just a few more steps. Copy me."

His mother took a step.
Copycub took a step.
His mother took another step.
Copycub took another step . . .
and another . . .
and another, until . . .

"We're here, Copycub!"
Behind a tumble of rocks was the entrance to the cave.

Soon they were inside.

The cave was quiet and dry, and carpeted with leaves.

Copycub's mother hugged him until he was warm.

"We're safe now," she said. "Soon we'll be sleeping tight, and when we wake up it'll be springtime again."

They watched the snow falling outside. Then they snuggled down into the leaves.

His mother yawned.
Copycub yawned.
His mother put her arms
around Copycub.
Copycub put his arms
around his mother.
His mother said,
"Goodnight, my little
Copycub. See you in
the springtime."
But Copycub didn't answer.

He was already asleep.